To all the little ones who take their time and go slowly. – K.D.

www.enchantedlionbooks.com

This work, published as part of a program of aid for publication,
received support from the Institut Français.
(Cet ouvrage a bénéficié du soutien des Programmes d'aide
à la publication de l'Institut français.)

First American edition published in 2013 by Enchanted Lion Books, 351 Van Brunt Street,
Brooklyn, New York 11231
© 2013 by Enchanted Lion Books for this English-language edition
Translated by Claudia Bedrick
Originally published in French by Éditions Frimousse as Moi D'Abord!
© 2010 Éditions Frimousse
Font "Penne" © Renaud Pennelle
ISBN 978-1-59270-136-0
Printed in April 2013 by South China Printing Company

ME FIRST!

Michaël Escoffier
Kris Di Giacomo

ENCHANTED LION BOOKS

NEW YORK

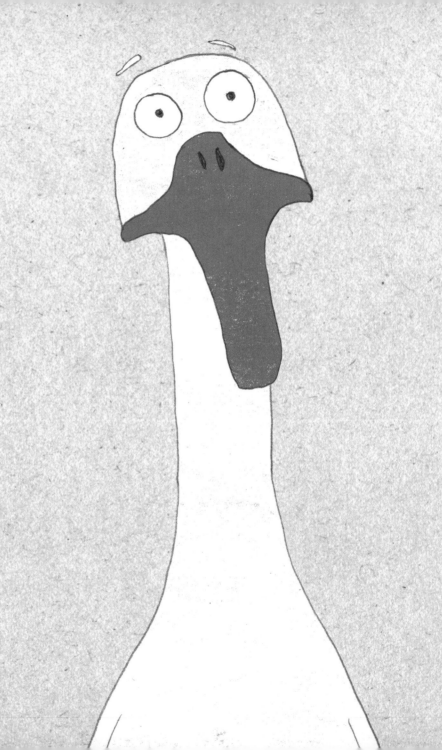

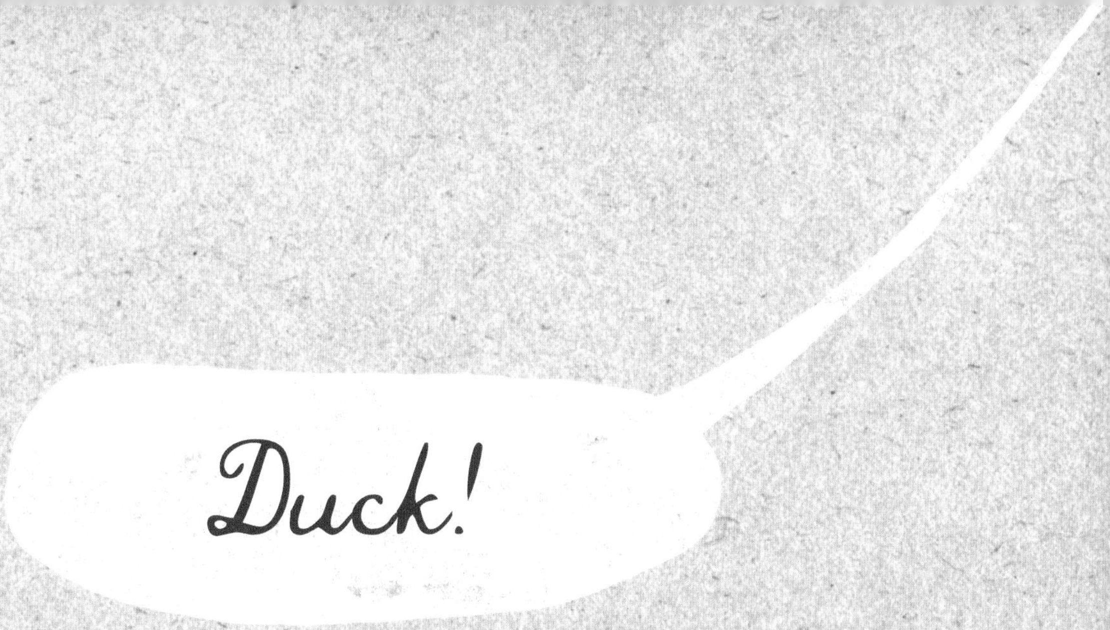
Duck!